This Little Hippo
book belongs to

_____

_____

Scholastic Children's Books,
Commonwealth House, 1-19 New Oxford Street
London WC1A 1NU, UK
a division of Scholastic Ltd

London ~ New York ~ Toronto ~ Sydney ~ Auckland
Mexico City ~ New Delhi ~ Hong Kong

First published in the UK in 2000 by Little Hippo, an imprint of Scholastic Ltd

Copyright © Adrienne Geoghegan 2000

ISBN 0 439 01170 1

Printed and bound in China

2 4 6 8 10 9 7 5 3 1

Who Needs POCKETS?

Adrienne Geoghegan

Little Hippo

Buddy collects things. Odd things.
So far he had a tinkle bell, a balloon,
a bottle of sweet-smelling perfume,
a funny poem and a key.

What he did not have was a pocket.

So he carried his collection between his teeth, only putting it down to eat or speak.

But soon he got tired of this and
he set out to look for a pocket.

Wa Wa Wa Wa Wa Wa Waaa

On his way, he met a cat.
"I'm lost, I'm lost!" cried the cat.
"My mother will never find me
without my tinkle bell."

Buddy was not too fond of cats.
They gave him the creeps.

But when he saw how sad this cat was, he gave him one of his favourite things . . .

. . . his tinkle bell.

"Oh, thank you," said the cat.
"Can I come with you?"
"Only if you're good at finding
pockets," replied Buddy.

So, the tinkle bell cat joined Buddy
in his search for a pocket for the
balloon, the sweet-smelling perfume,
the funny poem and the key.

On their way, they met . . .

. . . a duck.

"Excuse me, duck," said Buddy.
"Do you know where I can find
a pocket to put my things in?"
"Hiccup!" hicked the duck.

"Take your time," said Buddy. "Hiccup!" hicked the duck.

"Hold your breath and count to ten," said the cat. "Hiccup!" hicked the duck.

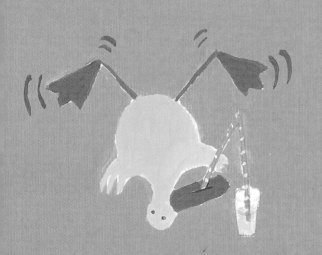

"Try a glass of water," said Buddy. "Hic . . . hic . . . hic hiccup!" hicked the duck.

"I know," said the cat, "blow up your balloon and give him a fright."
So Buddy blew up the balloon as fast as he could.

It
got
big,
BIGGER,
HUGE,
ENORMOUS
until . . .

BANG!

"QUACK! QUACK! QUACK!"
quacked the duck.
"At last!" said Buddy,
"No more hiccups!"
"Aren't I clever?" said
the cat.

Now Buddy had no balloon.
But he did have a quacky,
wacky duck friend to help
him find a pocket for his
sweet-smelling perfume,
his funny poem and his key.

Suddenly the three friends smelled a woeful smell.

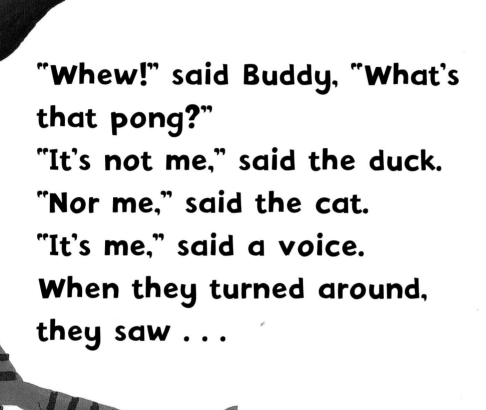

"Whew!" said Buddy, "What's that pong?"

"It's not me," said the duck.

"Nor me," said the cat.

"It's me," said a voice. When they turned around, they saw . . .

. . . a pig.

"I have no friends because of this, er, smell," she said.
"Squirt her with your perfume," said the cat.
"Yeah, go on," said the duck.
So Buddy sprayed the pig all over with the sweet-smelling perfume until there was none left.

Then the sweet-smelling pig joined
Buddy and the tinkle bell cat and
the quacky, wacky duck in their
search for a pocket for the funny
poem and the key.

They set off. Suddenly the
pig tripped and fell over.
When he looked down,
he saw a tortoise.

The tortoise was very
annoyed.

"Read him your funny
poem," said the cat.

"QUICK Buddy," said
the pig . . .

So Buddy read his funny poem out loud. The tortoise rolled over with laughter.

a ~~hilerius~~
~~hilaroios~~
~~redikeulis~~
ridiculous poem

"Wonderful! Marvellous! May I keep it?" asked the tortoise. "If you help us look for a pocket, you can," said Buddy.

So, the happy tortoise joined Buddy and the tinkle bell cat and the quacky, wacky duck and the sweet-smelling pig in their search for a pocket for the key.

On their way they came across a frantic rabbit.

"Help! Help! I'm locked out of my house and I have a cake in the oven!" he yelled.

"Calm down," said Buddy. He held out his key. "Would this work?"

"TRY IT! TRY IT!" cried the rabbit.
So he did. And it worked!
And the cake was saved!

"Can I keep the key?"
asked the rabbit.
"Ok," said Buddy. He went to pick up
his things but there was nothing left.

"Now that you are all here," said the
rabbit, "why not stay for tea?"

Buddy smiled. The duck quacked.
The cat tinkled. The tortoise laughed.
And the pig smelled almost as good
as the cake the rabbit baked.

They all sat down to eat.

"But Buddy," said the cat,
"we never found you a pocket."

"With friends like you," said Buddy.

"Who needs pockets?"